ABU ALI
Three Tales of the Middle East

ABU ALI
Three Tales of the Middle East

Retold by
Dorothy O. Van Woerkom

Illustrated by Harold Berson

Ready-to-Read

MACMILLAN PUBLISHING CO., INC.
New York
COLLIER MACMILLAN PUBLISHERS
London

Macmillan Publishing Co., Inc.
866 Third Avenue, New York, N.Y. 10022
Collier Macmillan Canada, Ltd.
Printed in the United States of America
10 9 8 7 6 5 4 3 2 1

LIBRARY OF CONGRESS CATALOGING IN PUBLICATION DATA
Van Woerkom, Dorothy.
  Abu Ali: three tales of the Middle East.

  (Ready-to-read)
  CONTENTS: Abu Ali counts his donkeys.—Abu Ali fools his friends.—Abu Ali fools himself.
  [1. Near East—Fiction.   2.   Short stories]
I. Berson, Harold.   II.   Title.
PZ7.V39Ab   [E]   76–8401
ISBN 0–02–791310–4

For Jane and Wayne

Contents

Abu Ali Counts His Donkeys

10

Abu Ali
bought nine donkeys
at the fair.
He climbed on
the first donkey.
"Whr-r-r-r!"
said Abu Ali.
The donkey
began to trot,
and the other
donkeys followed.

"Now,"
said Abu Ali,
"are all
my donkeys here?"

He turned around
and counted.
"One—two—three—
four—five—six—
seven—eight—
EIGHT donkeys!"

Abu Ali
jumped down
from his donkey.
He looked
behind trees,
behind bushes.
No donkey.

14

"I will count
again," he said.
"One—two—three—
four—five—six—
seven—eight—nine—
NINE donkeys!"

15

Abu Ali
climbed back
on his donkey.
"Whr-r-r-r!
Soon I will be home
with my nine
new donkeys."

CLIP,
CLAPPETY-CLOP.
CLIP,
CLAPPETY-CLOP.

"Now how many
donkeys do I have?"
Abu Ali counted
EIGHT donkeys!

He jumped down
from his donkey.
He looked
behind rocks,
over hilltops.
No donkey.

But when he
turned around—
NINE donkeys!
"When I get home,"
said Abu Ali,
"will I have
nine donkeys,
or will I
have eight?"

Abu Ali
saw his friend Musa
coming up the road.
"Help me, friend Musa!"
he cried.

"I keep losing
a donkey.
Now I have nine.
But when I climb
on my donkey
—like this—
I have only
eight donkeys!"

Musa laughed.
"Eight donkeys?
Nine donkeys?
Why, I see
TEN donkeys."

"Ten donkeys?"
said Abu Ali.
"Where do you see
ten donkeys?"

"I see eight donkeys
following your donkey.
I see the donkey
you are sitting on."
Musa
could not stop
laughing.

"Oh!"
said Abu Ali.
"I am sitting
on the ninth donkey!
But you said
you see ten."

"The tenth donkey
   is the donkey sitting
   on YOUR donkey,"
Musa said.
"Its name is
   Abu Ali!"

23

Abu Ali
Fools His
Friends

Three friends of Abu Ali
told tall tales about
how strong they were.

"But I am stronger
than you are, Hamid,"
Abu Ali said,
"and I am stronger
than Musa or Nouri."

"Show us," said Nouri.
"Yes," said Musa.
"What can you do?"

Abu Ali said,
"I can stay
out in the snow
all night without
heat or fire."

Musa laughed.
So did Hamid
and Nouri.
"But I can!"
said Abu Ali.
"If I can't, I will cook
a fine dinner for you!"

So Abu Ali
went out into the snow.
"Good night,"
said Hamid.
"Good luck,"
said Nouri.
"Don't freeze,"
Musa said.

The snow fell. The wind blew.

Soon everyone but Abu Ali was asleep.

How long the night was!

How dark, and how cold!

Across the street,
Abu Ali saw a candle
in a window.

How bright it looked.
How warm and friendly.
Abu Ali
watched the candle
all night long.

When the sun came up,
he went home to bed.

His friends
came to wake him up.
"Did you do it?"
Musa asked.

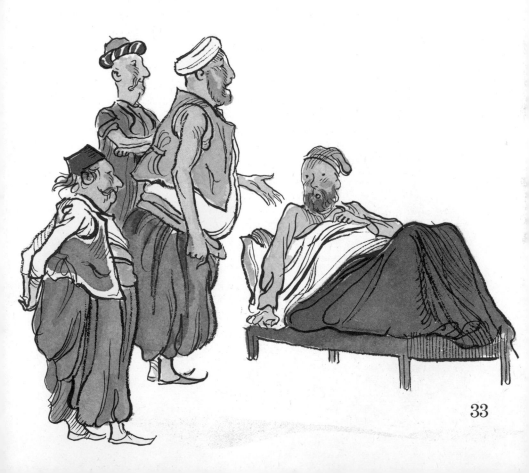

"Of course,"
said Abu Ali.
"But I was happy to see
a candle in the house
across the street."

"Oh?" Hamid said.

"A candle gives out heat!"

"You had heat?"
said Nouri.

"Then you must
cook our dinner!"

"All right, I will,"
said Abu Ali.
And he went
into his kitchen.

The three friends
waited...
and waited.
"Hurry, Ali!
We are hungry,"
Musa said.
"I cannot hurry, Musa."

37

Hamid, Musa and Nouri
went to see
why Abu Ali
could not hurry.

In the kitchen
they saw a pot
hanging from the ceiling.
On the floor
under the pot
they saw a candle.

"If a candle
gives out heat,"
said Abu Ali,
"then SOMEDAY
this candle will cook
your dinner!"

41

Abu Ali
Fools
Himself

Abu Ali was going
to Musa's house
for dinner.

On the way,
he stopped
to see Hamid.
"Friend Hamid,"
he said, "may I
wear your coat today?"

"Of course,"
 said Hamid.
"But why?"
"Because,"
 said Abu Ali,
"it has so many pockets."

46

Then Abu Ali

went to Musa's house.

"Come in, Ali!"

said Musa.

"Sit down.

Dinner is ready!"

"Thank you, Musa,"
said Abu Ali.
He took some meat.
"What fine meat," he said.
"Have some more,"
said Musa.

Abu Ali
took another
piece of meat.
He put it
in his pocket.

"Why did you do that?"
Musa asked.
"My coat is hungry,"
Abu Ali said.

"Have some bread,"
said Musa.
Abu Ali
took two loaves
of bread.
He put one loaf
in a pocket.

"Is your coat
still hungry?"
asked Musa.
"Oh, yes,"
said Abu Ali.
"This is a
very hungry coat!"

Abu Ali took two
bowls of rice.
He took two figs,
and two small cakes
with icing.

One of everything
went into a pocket
of the coat.

"Does your coat
want some water?"
Musa asked.
"No, thank you,"
said Abu Ali.
"This coat is
never thirsty."

When it was time
to leave,
Abu Ali said,
"Good-by, Musa.
Thank you
for the fine dinner."

"Good-by, Ali," Musa said.
"And good-by to your coat."

Abu Ali
hurried home.
"I will not
cook tomorrow,"
he said.
"My dinner is in
these pockets."

He put the coat
on a hook
and took a nap.

Hamid came by.

"Friend Ali?" said Hamid.

"I need my coat."

But Abu Ali
was asleep.
Hamid took his coat.
It was heavy.

"What a fine friend
Ali is!" said Hamid.

"I lend him my coat,
    and he fills my pockets
    with good things
    for me to eat!"